For the seasons, and all things that change—Mo

For Aimee and Addy and their canine friends,
Gracie, Grant, Cary, and Angel—Jon

# city dog, country frog

words Mo Willems • pictures Jon J Muth

Hyperion Books for Children | New York

spring

City Dog didn't stop on
that first day in the country;
he ran as far and
as fast as he could

and all without a leash!

City Dog spotted something he
had never seen, sitting on a rock.
(It was Country Frog.)

"What are you doing?" asked City Dog.

"Waiting for a friend," replied
Country Frog with a smile.

"But *you'll* do."

City Dog and Country Frog
played together.

City Dog was new to the country,
so Country Frog taught him
Country Frog games.

Country Frog's games involved
jumping and splashing and croaking.

That was spring.

summer

City Dog didn't stop
to admire the green, green grass;
he ran straight for
Country Frog's rock.

"I am going to do you a favor,"
said City Dog when
he found Country Frog.

"I am going to teach you
City Dog games."

City Dog's games involved
sniffing and fetching and barking.

City Dog and Country Frog played
until Country Frog was too tired
to sniff and fetch and bark

anymore.

That was summer.

fall

City Dog didn't stop
to sniff the falling leaves;
he ran straight
for Country Frog's rock.

"What shall we play today?" asked City Dog.
"Dog or Frog games?"

Country Frog took a deep breath.

"I am a tired frog," replied Country Frog.
"Maybe we can play remember-ing games."

City Dog and Country Frog
sat together on the rock.

They remembered their spring
jumping and splashing and croaking.

They remembered their summer
sniffing and fetching and barking.

That was fall.

winter

City Dog didn't stop
to eat the snow;
he ran straight for
Country Frog's rock.

City Dog looked for Country Frog.

Country Frog was not there.

That was winter.

spring again

Country Chipmunk spotted something she had never seen, sitting on a rock.

(It was City Dog.)

"What are you doing?"
asked Country Chipmunk.

"Waiting for a friend,"
replied City Dog sadly.

Then he smiled a
froggy smile and said . . .

"But *you'll* do."

That
was
spring
again.